A two twirl
CHRISTMAS
AN EAGLE ELITE SHORT

A two twirl CHRISTMAS

AN EAGLE ELITE SHORT

RACHEL VAN DYKEN

#1 *NEW YORK TIMES*
BESTSELLING AUTHOR

To my Readers
who have stuck with me for so long

CHAPTER ONE

Sergio

Tears burned the back of my eyes when I finally glanced at the field. It took me around forty minutes to finally make my way outside on Christmas evening and another two hours to finally walk my way around the massive house and look up at the night sky.

So many stars and I had to wonder if she was up there somehow looking down at all of us.

I'd be doing her a favor by killing her. The words tasted so bitter and hateful in my mouth that I felt like shit all over again.

"Everyone is afraid of dying. The hardest part is never admitting we're mortal but coming to terms with the fact that we have no control over how long we're given. You. Do."

"No… I don't. You're trying to take that control."

"Say the word." My hand moved to the Glock strapped to my thigh.

"I'm not afraid." Her lips trembled. *"At least not of death… but I am afraid of something."*

"Oh yeah?" I hissed. *"What's that?"*

"Yours."

Confused, I stepped back, immediately looking for a weapon. "I don't understand."

"You wouldn't."

I remembered that day like it was yesterday, sitting by the fire, thinking about death, wondering what the whole point was about this life, literally feeling the itching from the tally mark tattoo scarring on my ribs, and wondering if she would just be one more.

And she would.

Just not in the way I thought.

I squeeze my eyes closed.

A hand clasped hard on my shoulder. "It will never get easier."

"That was a horrible pep talk," I muttered, knowing immediately it was Chase that had chosen to come out with me.

"He sucks at them." Phoenix's voice came next. "But at least he's here and not upstairs with—"

"—Kids? Because they're driving me insane." Chase laughed. "Wouldn't want it any other way."

"Never." Tex joined in.

How many of them had come out for this moment? For this celebration? I'd always done it by myself. I guess they realized it was ten years since she'd left us.

Left me.

I'd thought I was so old at the time, but I'd been an idiot, so young, so stupid, so ridiculously arrogant about the ways of this life and this world. And she'd seen it so clearly that even to this day, it's almost embarrassing, maybe because she had so much pain that she recognized it in others. She knew I was a boy trying to be a man—but that's what she did to me... she made me a man.

I'd like to think she made me a good husband and a good father, even though I might actually murder my future son-in-laws one day if they talk shit to me. And yet, I'm stupidly smiling at the fact that my little girls will get their happily ever after, one that took me at least one try to get right, not because I chose wrong but because the universe had something different in store.

And sometimes. Sometimes it's important to remember that life isn't fair, and we shouldn't expect it to be.

When life fails you, the temptation is always to fight first, and then once the fight leaves, you want to give up because you've spent so long fighting and trying to look strong to everyone else, yourself included. You look in the mirror, and you say: *I'm okay, I'm okay, I'm okay.*

And all it fucking takes is one person who you know truly cares to walk up to you and ask, "Hey man, you doin' good? You okay?"

To mentally and spiritually break. Sometimes the reaction is anger out of the desperation you feel, and other times you just lose it because you're at your breaking point and you can't lie to yourself or others anymore. It's when your throat gets clogged, your chest starts to pound and tighten all at once, and tears burn the back of your eyes, but the more you try to hold it in, the worse it gets over and over and over again, like a sickness taking hold, it consumes you to the point of feeling like you may never come back from it.

But your body needs it. It needs a cleansing. It needs something that's going to tell it that it's okay to grieve.

It's okay to let go.

Let. It. Go.

The guys next to me were *those guys.*

My wife was *that woman.*

My family saved me from losing myself to that grief.

And the sky, the sunrise—well, that was Andi the entire time, wasn't it? Helping me day in and day out when the dark clouds poured.

"It's supposed to snow," Nixon's voice chimed in.

"You sure?" Dante asked, approaching. I can hear his footsteps crunching; his voice is more distant.

"Doubtful," Andrei said, his voice low. "There aren't enough clouds."

"Stars," I answered thoughtfully. "There are stars."

Everyone was silent.

"You didn't have to all come, you know," I whispered. "I know it's close to the anniversary, and I always promised her I would—"

I couldn't finish my thought.

Several hands touched my back and shoulders… messed with my hair.

And then Phoenix's deep voice rang out. "You promised to visit the trees you planted for her. Wasn't that something she always teased you about? A Christmas tree farm? I think we should finally go visit them. After all, Frank and Luca have been bothering the shit out of all of us about not seeing all the hard work they're doing."

I couldn't tell if my laughter was out of nervousness or ridiculousness that two crazy retired mob bosses spent their days at a Christmas tree farm, golfing, playing chess, and wine tasting, but life can be stranger than fiction, isn't that the saying?

Taking a deep breath, I finally truly opened my eyes and stared at the field straight ahead of me. It was so different now.

It had life.

When it used to only remind me of death.

So many trees were scattered around that it was hardly recognizable from that morning she left us.

"Let's go see the trees." Throat thick, I started walking.

Toward Andi's trees.

Because in her death, on that field, staring up at the sky, I wanted to create life.

For her memory.

For mine.

For future generations.

She would live on over and over again.

The point was… Andi would live.

CHAPTER TWO

Val

He was out there. I could see the flashlight and even the way his posture was rigid. He always tried to be so strong, but I often reminded him that it's okay to be weak. Only in weakness can you find your strength.

I was a firm believer that when you ask for more, you're given less to teach you how to learn to deal with more. When you ask for strength, you'll immediately feel weak because how else can you freaking possibly learn to be strong over and over again unless you've hit rock bottom?

I remembered watching an Instagram Reel about it once, about how the opposite is sometimes true when you need the other more.

Not because the Universe hates you.

But because it needs to refine you to make you the best version of yourself you could possibly be.

Sergio's the best of the best. I swear I could tell him that every second of every day, and he would still find at least two things he was a failure at that he needed to work at.

It used to drive me crazy until I realized it was his way of constantly bettering himself, nobody's perfect, not even the great Sergio Abandonato.

I touched the window with my fingertips. It was the same room she stayed in. I often went there and talked with her. Told her how I was doing, how married life was, motherhood…

All of it.

And during the holidays, it's like magic came over that room—most holiday nights when I was standing at that window when it was time…

It snowed.

Which I guess wasn't rare for Chicago.

So maybe I was being hopeful it would snow tonight for Sergio.

For the Christmas farm.

For her.

I could see the lights from the giant building that Luca just had to have on the edge of the property with twinkle lights, a wine bar, and a coffee bar just in case they were out there too long, which they always were during the winter like they were paying homage, or maybe just honoring a life lost.

Rare, I guess, in the mafia, to feel sadness for others doesn't seem like something that's possibly even accurate.

But that's the Five Families.

Every other mafia can suck it because ours is real—it's blood, it's true, and it's based on something that nobody can ever break.

Blood.

Loyalty.

Family.

And no book, no tv show, no movie, would ever be able to hold a candle to what we have, to our truth.

I could have sworn in that moment, watching Sergio look up at the sky with the guys around him, then look back toward the building.

I felt something.

A presence?

Maybe it was my imagination, but it made me smile.

"He's doing great," I whispered.

While the wind whispered right back, "So are you."

I smiled at the window one last time, touched it with my fingertips, leaving tiny little smudge marks on the glass, and looked away.

The moment was too precious for me to witness.

He'd been waiting a long time for it, and so had I, both of us for different reasons, and right now he needed the men around him, and I was okay with waiting, waiting for my husband to come back to the house, waiting for him to kiss me goodnight and make love to me in the morning.

I was his.

And he, while it felt like at one time was given to me—was well and truly mine. I adored him with every inch of my body and soul.

I just needed to prepare myself for whatever sadness would come out of that forest of trees with him.

I would endure it for his sake.

I would accept it for hers.

I would own it for mine.

Smiling, I walked out of the room and clicked the door shut as laughter hit my ears from the kitchen downstairs. My friends and family were all there, except for a few of the bosses.

All the kids, cousins, wives.

My footsteps became stronger as I walked down those stairs one at a time, taking the same journey I knew Andi and Sergio had taken all those years ago.

I felt the ghost of her. I smiled and touched the banister and took each step one at a time, imagining how hard that walk must have been for her, how devastating and yet beautiful to walk into the presence of the sunrise, knowing without a doubt that the love of your life would be mere footsteps behind you, always your shadow, always allowing you to face the world on your own, but willing to step in whenever you called his name.

What a beautiful end after such a tragic beginning.

I touched my chest and smiled, and I kept walking.

I stopped when I was midway down the stairs, and I looked up at the two massive skylights that Sergio had refused to take down—his reasoning was that Andi always looked up—even in the end—and how sad to have that view obstructed by the ceiling? When the stars are enormously forever?

I took another step after looking back down and finally made it to the main level and walked into the kitchen. Everyone was laughing and smiling.

It was exactly how she would have wanted it.

No matter the circumstances, she wanted people to live.

I'd like to believe that in that messy kitchen with wine, chicken nuggets, pasta, and yelling—she got her last wish.

CHAPTER THREE

Sergio

I stared up at the sky before taking another step. I didn't just feel Andi... I felt Val. I looked over my shoulder and could have sworn I felt her right there, holding my hand, telling me to keep walking.

You see, in Andi leaving, I found a second chance, a gift, a family. Something I know she always wanted me to have even if she couldn't or wouldn't be able to.

In those last moments, I prayed so hard for a miracle.

I asked why so many times.

And my answer was always silence.

I hated the universe. I hated everyone, and then I realized that sometimes the peace was in the silence, not the immediate answer. Silence gave you patience, it gave you trust, it forced you to continue to fight through the mud in order to get to the end of whatever battle you were facing.

In the end, you see, silence always answered, just not in the way you often wanted it to.

"I would kill for a snowmobile right now," Tex muttered.

I laughed out loud; it felt good. My lungs breathed in the cold winter air, my eyes watered, and I could see my breath puff out in front of my face. "It's just a bit of snow."

"It's literally a foot," Tex answered. "I counted."

"What? You literally pulled out a yardstick, dumbass?" Nixon asked.

Chase burst out laughing. "He probably keeps it to measure something else with it."

Nixon swore. "My sister, he's married to my sister."

Andrei cursed and fell on his knees, then got up. "Tell anyone that happened, and I'm getting the tiger."

Phoenix huffed out a breath next to me. "Wait, you told me Tony died!"

Andrei shrugged. "I lied."

"He does that often." Nixon nodded. "All right, just another fifty freaking miles, and we're there."

Dante laughed. "It's five hundred feet."

"Oh, what? Now you have a measuring stick?" Tex snorted.

Dante pointed to his head. "No, I have a brain. You should try growing one, old man."

Tex lunged for him and nearly fell on his knees. "Come here!"

Dante leaped into the air and laughed. "Old Tex Donald had a farm—"

"—Someone tackle him." Tex chased after him but was

clearly too slow and then just gave up once Dante was so far ahead of us.

"I love him yet hate him. It's weird." Chase finally broke the silence and put his hand back on my shoulder. "You ready to see the rest of the trees?"

We were right in front of the entire Christmas miracle of a forest, the trees weren't huge, but they were good enough size. The trees were all placed in the form of a star, pointing toward the most beautiful tree there.

Andi's.

Two figures started walking toward us, both of them in black peacoats, one with a red scarf and the other with a green one.

Nixon sighed out loud. "It's like... they want us to comment on how wrong and weird it is for old bosses to look... like that."

"Swear if he had a cat sweater, I'd be out." Chase crossed his arms and then snapped his fingers. "Hey, perfect gift, a cat sweater."

Tex nodded. "Or just get him like a naked cat and call it Stan Lee."

"Huh?" Chase asked.

Tex grinned and pointed ahead. "They look like men who would enjoy a nice naked—"

"—DO NOT..." Dante, who we'd caught up to, covered his ears. "...finish that sentence."

"Ah, the younger ones," Phoenix said, sharing a smile with Andrei.

I waited until Luca and Frank were right in front of me. I didn't break down, and I didn't do anything other than stare straight ahead.

Toward the middle of the forest.

Her tree.

"I think I need to go alone this time. Can you guys just give me five minutes?" I didn't dare look at any of them because I was afraid I'd burst into tears and collapse in the snow in front of everyone. I hadn't done that since *that* morning, just allowed myself to be vulnerable and scream at the world while knowing that beauty happened in all phases of life, in all areas, even in darkness and pain, beauty could co-exist.

I took a deep breath, followed by another.

"Go," Luca finally said. "We'll meet you in a few minutes."

I didn't answer. I just stared straight ahead at the prettiest tree in the lot. My boots crunched against the snow. *I passed gorgeous trees, full of life, that had everything going for them… that people would probably pay hundreds for.*

I touched them with my black leather gloved hands as I walked, and when it felt too cold, too empty and isolated, I let the cold hit me and make me feel alive.

Maybe because a part of me was breathing and existing for her too.

The closer I got, the darker it felt. I'd purposefully told Luca and Frank not to put lights on her tree. It felt wrong to add artificial lights to something that, in my mind, would always shine on its own.

As it got darker, I got warmer.

Finally, I stopped in front of the tree and unwrapped the scarf around my neck—a gift from my wife.

She knit in it, *Two Twirls*.

It was our first anniversary after getting married, and my wife's gift to me was the memory of another. I wondered if that's how you know you've found a soul mate… when they fully understand that it's okay to love more than one person and have them in your soul for eternity. You see, you don't ever forget that love, you just make room for more—the heart has incredible abilities.

Mine held two.

A memory of one.

The life of another.

Two souls.

One heart.

With shaking hands, I wrapped the scarf around the tree. I had to kneel down to do it, after all, the rest of the trees had been here a long time. We'd planted them after her death, it had been my idea to make a star.

But something had always been missing, and I realized what was missing last year as I did my yearly Christmas walk through the trees. It was Andi.

She was somehow still missing.

So we planted a new tree.

It was smaller than the others but no less powerful and beautiful.

It stood around a foot tall and had a dusting of fresh snow on it. It lacked any sort of decorations or Christmas lights, and yet if I had to pick one tree out of the entire lot.

It would be this one. Because a small tree by itself in the cold without anything—seemed so very brave, just like Andi.

"You're beautiful," I said after wrapping the scarf around the tree. I stayed on my knees, touched the pine needles, and smiled. "And very small, but you always were short." The needles were sharp. "Looks about right, little tree. I hope one day, when you grow big enough, that you'll remember you don't have to be anything but yourself, that you're good enough as a tiny tree, good enough as a huge tree. I hope you live, even if it's not the way either of us wanted. Live."

Tears started to stream down my cheeks, but I didn't brush them away. I let them hit the snow by the base of the tree, and minutes later when I heard the crunch of footsteps as the men behind me came over. I looked up.

It had started to snow.

CHAPTER FOUR

Val

It was snowing. My girls were napping.

I smiled and took a sip of my hot tea; it burned down my throat in a good way, making me warm and comforted.

I loved the way the chaos surrounded me. It wouldn't last long; I wasn't dumb. Suddenly someone shouted, "SNOW!" and started running outside without shoes.

Probably one of Chase's kids, let's be honest.

Or maybe even Serena. She was a wild one.

Junior started running too, and then it was absolute madness as everyone in the kitchen suddenly left; even the moms were running out there to make sure nobody decided it would be a good idea to forget gloves and jackets.

"You coming?" Trace stopped at the door to the backyard. I could tell by her face that she knew my answer would be no. She simply nodded her head and said, "Merry Christmas, Val. He loves you. I hope you always remember that. No matter who had him first, you have him now. You're his soul."

I smiled. "Trace, I'm okay with sharing his soul. I'd prefer it that way. It makes him stronger, braver, a better husband and father—sharing his soul doesn't make me jealous. Sometimes life throws things at us like this, and my story... I think it was supposed to be like this, not because I'm strong, but because the weakest of us need challenges and love. And I loved her too, so in a way, we love him together in different times when he has needed our love the most."

A tear slid down Trace's cheek. She quickly brushed it away with her glove. "You're wrong."

"What?" I frowned.

Her smile was faint. "You're so strong, Val. So very strong, even then, even more so now."

The front door shut. The sound of the guys talking filled the room.

She grinned at me. "I'm going to go find my inner Elsa and build a snowman, and you, you should probably go find your man. I'm sure he'll want you."

I shrugged. "Even if he needs to be alone. I've got the snow. I've got my family. And he'll come when he's ready."

Nixon poked his head into the kitchen and shook off his jacket. "Who's coming?"

"Santa." Trace deadpanned. "And put that jacket back on; your daughter just ran out there in a tank top."

"Son of a bitch!" Nixon roared. "Serena, get back in here!"

I frowned. "She was wearing a sweater?"

"I know." Trace laughed. "I just feel like it's extremely healthy to continuously get his blood pumping."

I pointed at my head. "Smart woman."

"They don't call me boss for nothing." She winked. "OH, I mean him… definitely him."

I busted out laughing. "Sureeee."

She winked and shut the door as Nixon made a beeline toward a fully clothed Serena yelling at the top of his lungs to get dressed before she caught a cold or the flu, and then somehow, I heard him add in chickenpox, but I think he was just worried?

I set my mug down, shoved my chair back, and felt him before he even said anything.

A hand lay on my right shoulder, and the other followed on my left. I simply leaned back into his arms. He was so warm, so alive.

My eyes squeezed shut. "How was the tree?"

"Small." He kissed my neck. "I gave it the scarf."

A tear ran down my cheek. "Hopefully, the tree stays warm for Christmas and grows really big one day."

"I have no doubt it will," he said, slowly turning me in his arms and holding me against him. "I love you."

I grinned up at him. "I love you too."

"I really, really, really…" He kissed my nose. "Love you. Adore you. Cherish you. Lust for you. Need you. If you get tired of hearing it, I don't give a shit because I love you. You anchor me, you make me feel everything all the time, the good, the bad, but mostly, you are so selfless, beautiful." He tilted my chin toward him with his gloved fingers. "You're my best friend, Val. I know our story is different, but I truly wouldn't want anyone else by my side."

I wanted to say even Andi, but that felt petty and wrong.

He smiled down at me. "She was at my side for a season. You're at my side for forever. Both had different meanings, different needs, and right now. I need you."

I squeezed my eyes shut to keep the tears from pouring down my face. I missed her too. Nobody ever really asked me about it, but I know he knew; I just didn't want to make things weird.

Sometimes I felt her presence like a breath of wind through the trees.

"I need you too." I licked my lips, then reached up and pressed a kiss to his.

He smiled against my parted mouth and slipped his tongue past my bottom lip, lightly kissing me and then pulling back. "Let's go upstairs. Nixon and Trace are on babysitting duty along with Tex."

Of course, Tex chose that moment to walk by us with a shovel and start yelling at the top of his lungs not to disturb the bodies in the backyard.

Kids screamed.

Nixon cursed.

Merry Christmas?

I laughed against Sergio's chest. "You Abandonatos are out of control."

Chase sprinted through the kitchen. "Did the duck get loose?"

"What duck?" Sergio asked in a way calmer voice.

Chase's eyes widened. "The one for Christmas dinner, you idiot!"

"You mean the goose?" I asked.

"Oh shit." Chase disappeared in a sprint toward Nixon.

"We had a goose?"

Sergio shrugged. "I thought it was a turkey."

Nixon held out his shovel in the backyard, Chase dogged it.

Phoenix, Dante, and Andrei finally came in, yawning and high fiving.

"What did you guys do?" I asked.

Phoenix grinned. "The goose needed to be set free."

"It was a turkey." Dante nodded.

"Technically, we got a goose, a turkey, and a duck and played a prank on both Nixon and Chase to see how long it would take them to fight. Oh shit, they have shovels!" Phoenix ran.

Andrei started pulling hundreds out of his pocket, and the door slammed behind them.

"Yeah," I laughed. "I think they got it totally under control."

Sergio stared out the window and winced as the shovel flew toward Chase. "Yeah, completely calm."

"Almost serene." I nodded.

"Yup." He picked me up in his arms. "Now, let's go do the opposite of that."

"Shovel throwing?"

"Calm." He winked. "I want to taste you. All of you. Now."

"I might taste like snow, sweat, tears, and worry."

"I might kiss it all away; you should just let me."

I nodded. "Okay."

"Okay." He pressed a kiss to my neck. "Let's go."

CHAPTER FIVE

Sergio

Val had always been my rock, even when she didn't realize it, even when she annoyed the hell out of me when I first met her. She'd been so young, and I'd felt like I'd aged across lifetimes. I'd been so lost in my own grief that it took someone like her kissing me and telling me to get it together to snap me out of it, and even then, I was pissed off because she wasn't intimidated by me at all, she challenged me, she kissed me first.

That movie theater was both the best and worst decision of my life, the best because it changed me, the worst because I've only ever been that afraid once, and that was in the field we planted the trees.

I grabbed her hand and walked her toward the stairs; the laughter from the rest of the family started to fade. All I had was her hand.

It was all I needed.

How many times had I mourned going down those stairs, only to go back up those same stairs holding my wife's hand?

The plan I'd had so long ago wasn't the same.

It was different.

Then again, Andi had been different, just like Val. Both molded me into the man I was today, and I wouldn't trade that for anything.

She squeezed my hand tight. "I missed you."

I stopped walking up the stairs and pulled her against me. "I wasn't gone long."

Her smile was slightly sad. "It wasn't the time you were gone, Sergio. It was that I was loaning you to someone else for a while. I wasn't jealous. Okay, maybe a little bit, but I genuinely missed you and your touch, your hand."

"Do you realize…" I asked. "…how big my love is for you?"

"Bigger than the stars?" She laughed and started to walk away, tugging me with her.

I pulled her back. "Bigger." I kissed the back of her head and held her against me. "So much bigger."

She relaxed against me; her hair smelled like coconuts and almonds. I inhaled and hugged her even tighter.

Val turned in my arms and pressed a kiss to my neck. It was rare in this business to actually relax for one minute, let alone longer than that, but she always had this way of making me feel like I could exist just in the space between us.

"Hey." She reached for my jeans, tugged at the button, and undid it. "I need you."

I laughed. "Eager?"

"I want an early Christmas present."

"And my dick is your present?"

"Absolutely." She grinned and easily pushed me toward the bedroom. I was shoved onto the bed—eagerly. I kicked off my jeans in the same way, and when her dark hair fell against my thighs, and her lips descended toward my cock—I looked down and laughed. "You know you used to get embarrassed when—"

"Shhhh." She pressed a finger to my lips and then lowered her mouth.

With a curse, I lifted my hips as she sucked me dry, nearly choking herself in the process. "You're too good at this."

She pulled back and winked. "I know. I just figured that this was a day to celebrate."

"Christmas?"

"Life." She pulled off her top, then her bra, and lowered her body onto mine. "Life, Sergio."

"I love you," I whispered, tears in my eyes that I didn't want to shed because I would never want Val to think that it was because I missed Andi—even though I did—my heart had space for two.

And I knew in my soul Val knew that as well.

"Hey." Val leaned down; my fingers tugged at her leggings, pulling the rest of her clothes off. "It's okay to miss her too."

"I know."

"I know." She repeated back. "And my heart will always have space for you."

"Mine too."

"Good." Val pressed another soft kiss to my mouth and whispered, "Now, let's celebrate."

"However will we do that?" I joked.

She impaled herself on me.

"Shit." I coughed out. "So violent."

"So good." She laughed. "Now let me love you."

"Done." I took a deep breath as she rode me slowly. "Done. For you. Always done."

"Two twirls."

"Two twirls," I repeated as I always did every Christmas, not as a reminder of Andi, but as a reminder of life, of living, of loving.

Of us.

Because every Christmas should include—not one but two twirls.

THANK YOU!

Thank you to every person who has supported this series.
You guys are amazing,
I'm so thankful to my readers and my team.
You guys are awesome.

merry christmas

WANT MORE RVD?

Did you enjoy
A *two twirl* CHRISTMAS?
Then check out these other Mafia Romances!

The Eagle Elite World encompasses three separate series
that can each be read on its own:

EAGLE ELITE (Italian Mafia)
ELITE BRATVA BROTHERHOOD (Russian Mafia)
MAFIA *Royals* (the next generation).

Flip the page,
pick a couple you want to know more about,
and enjoy!

EAGLE ELITE
New Adult, Mafia Romance — Interconnected Standalones
Elite (Nixon & Trace's story)
Elect (Nixon & Trace's story)
Entice (Chase & Mil's story)
Elicit (Tex & Mo's story)
Bang Bang (Axel & Amy's story)
Enforce (Elite + from the boys' POV)
Ember (Phoenix & Bee's story)
Elude (Sergio & Andi's story)
Empire (Sergio & Val's story)
Enrage (Dante & El's story)
Eulogy (Chase & Luciana's story)
Exposed (Dom & Tanit's story)
Envy (Vic & Renee's story)

ELITE BRATVA BROTHERHOOD
New Adult, Mafia Romance — Interconnected Standalones
RIP (Nikolai & Maya's story)
Debase (Andrei & Alice's story)
Dissolution (Santino & Katya's story)

MAFIA ROYALS ROMANCES
New Adult, Mafia Romance — Interconnected Standalones
Royal Bully (Asher & Claire's story)
Ruthless Princess (Serena & Junior's story)
Scandalous Prince (Breaker & Violet's story)
Destructive King (Asher & Annie's story)
Mafia King (Tank & Kartini's story)
Fallen Royal (Maksim & Izzy's Story)
Broken Crown (King & Del's story)

ABOUT THE AUTHOR

Rachel Van Dyken is the #1 *New York Times*, *Wall Street Journal*, and *USA Today* bestselling author of over 100 books ranging from new adult romance to mafia romance to paranormal & fantasy romance. With over four million copies sold, she's been featured in *Forbes*, *US Weekly*, and *USA Today*. Her books have been translated into more than 15 countries. She was one of the first romance authors to have a Kindle in Motion book through Amazon publishing and continues to strive to be on the cutting edge of the reader experience. She keeps her home in the Pacific Northwest with her husband, adorable sons, a naked cat, and two dogs. For more information about her books and upcoming events, visit www.RachelVanDykenAuthor.com.

ALSO BY RACHEL VAN DYKEN

EAGLE ELITE
New Adult, Mafia Romance — Interconnected Standalones
Elite (Nixon & Trace's story)
Elect (Nixon & Trace's story)
Entice (Chase & Mil's story)
Elicit (Tex & Mo's story)
Bang Bang (Axel & Amy's story)
Enforce (Elite+ from the boys' POV)
Ember (Phoenix & Bee's story)
Elude (Sergio & Andi's story)
Empire (Sergio & Val's story)
Enrage (Dante & El's story)
Eulogy (Chase & Luciana's story)
Exposed (Dom & Tanit's story)
Envy (Vic & Renee's story)

ELITE BRATVA BROTHERHOOD
New Adult, Mafia Romance — Interconnected Standalones
RIP (Nikolai & Maya's story)
Debase (Andrei & Alice's story)
Dissolution (Santino & Katya's story)

MAFIA ROYALS ROMANCES
New Adult, Mafia Romance — Interconnected Standalones
Royal Bully (Asher & Claire's story)
Ruthless Princess (Serena & Junior's story)
Scandalous Prince (Breaker & Violet's story)
Destructive King (Asher & Annie's story)
Mafia King (Tank & Kartini's story)
Fallen Royal (Maksim & Izzy's Story)
Broken Crown (King & Del's story)

RACHEL VAN DYKEN & M. ROBINSON
New Adult, Romantic Suspense — Interconnected Standalones
Mafia Casanova (Romeo & Eden's story)
Falling for the Villain (Juliet Sinacore's story)

STANDALONE ROMANCES
New Adult, Angsty Romance — Standalone Novels
The Perfects (Ambrose & Mary-Belle's story)
The Unperfects (Quinn's Story)

CRUEL SUMMER TRILOGY
New Adult, Angsty Romance — Trilogy
Summer Heat (Marlon & Ray's story)
Summer Seduction (Marlon & Ray's story)
Summer Nights (Marlon & Ray's story)

STANDALONE K-POP ROMANCES
New Adult, Angsty, Rockstar Romances — Standalone Novels
My Summer In Seoul (Grace's story)
The Anti-Fan & The Idol

WINGMEN INC.
New Adult, Romantic Comedies — Interconnected Standalones
The Matchmaker's Playbook (Ian & Blake's story)
The Matchmaker's Replacement (Lex & Gabi's story)

LIARS, INC
New Adult, Romantic Comedies — Interconnected Standalones
Dirty Exes (Colin, Jessie & Blaire's story)
Dangerous Exes (Jessie & Isla's story)

CURIOUS LIAISONS
New Adult, Romantic Comedies — Interconnected Standalones
Cheater (Lucas & Avery's story)
Cheater's Regret (Thatch & Austin's story)

STANDALONE DRAMEDY
RomCom with Dramatic Moments — Standalone Novel
The Godparent Trap (Rip & Colby's story)

THE BET SERIES
New Adult, Romantic Comedies — Interconnected Standalones
The Bet (Travis & Kacey's story)
The Wager (Jake & Char Lynn's story)
The Dare (Jace & Beth Lynn's story)

THE BACHELORS OF ARIZONA
New Adult Romances — Interconnected Standalones
The Bachelor Auction (Brock & Jane's story)
The Playboy Bachelor (Bentley & Margot's story)
The Bachelor Contract (Brant & Nikki's story)

KATHY IRELAND & RACHEL VAN DYKEN
Women's Fiction — Standalone
Fashion Jungle

STANDALONE ROMANCES
Romantic Comedy, Holiday Romance — Standalone Novel
A Crown for Christmas (Fitz & Phillipa's story)
New Adult, Romantic Comedies — Standalone Novels
Every Girl Does It (Preston & Amanda's story)
Compromising Kessen (Christian & Kessen's story)
New Adult, Fantasy Romance — Standalone Novel
Divine Uprising (Athena & Adonis's story)
Inspirational, Historical Romance — Standalone Novel
The Parting Gift — written with Leah Sanders (Blaine and Mara's story)

RACHEL VAN DYKEN & LEAH SANDERS
WALTZING WITH THE WALLFLOWER
Regency Romances — Interconnected Standalones
Waltzing with the Wallflower (Ambrose & Cordelia)
Beguiling Bridget (Anthony & Bridget's story)
Taming Wilde (Colin & Gemma's story)

LONDON FAIRY TALES
Fairy Tale Inspired Regency Romances —
Interconnected Standalones
Upon a Midnight Dream (Stefan & Rosalind's story)
Whispered Music (Dominique & Isabelle's story)
The Wolf's Pursuit (Hunter & Gwendolyn's story)
When Ash Falls (Ashton & Sofia's story)

RENWICK HOUSE
Regency Romances — Interconnected Standalones
The Ugly Duckling Debutante (Nicholas & Sara's story)
The Seduction of Sebastian St. James (Sebastian & Emma's story)
The Redemption of Lord Rawlings (Phillip & Abigail's story)
An Unlikely Alliance (Royce & Evelyn's story)
The Devil Duke Takes a Bride (Benedict & Katherine's story)

www.rachelvandykenauthor.com